SERIOUS GRAFFITI

Other books by Barbara Mitchelhill

DAMIAN DROOTH
SUPERSLEUTH

SERIOUS GRAFFITI

BARBARA
MITCHELHILL

Illustrated by TONY ROSS

For Max and Tom Scott and their
mum and dad, with much love.
B.M.

First published in Great Britain in 2007
by Andersen Press Limited, 20 Vauxhall Bridge Road, London SW1V 2SA
www.andersenpress.co.uk

Reprinted 2007

British Library Cataloguing in Publication Data available.

ISBN 978 184 270 6503

Printed in the UK by CPI Bookmarque, Croydon, CR0 4TD

Chapter 1

You probably know my name. I'm Damian Drooth Supersleuth and Ace Detective. I've solved loads of crimes but let me tell you about one that happened at our school. It was dead exciting. The head teacher couldn't solve it. The police couldn't solve it. But in the end, I solved it.

I first learned of the crime during our maths lesson, last Thursday when the head, Mr Spratt, came marching into our classroom. I could tell straight away he was in a real temper. When he's like that, he peers over his glasses – and he was peering over them now.

'I have something serious to tell you

all,' he said to the class. 'Someone has sprayed paint on the walls of the boys' lavatories. This graffiti is quite disgraceful as the decorators have only just finished painting. Now it will have to be done again.'

He peered over the top of his glasses,

fixing everybody with his beady black eyes.

'I want the person responsible to come to my office before the end of school tomorrow or...' we waited to hear the terrible news, '...or the whole school will be punished.'

A gasp rippled round the room.

'That's not fair, sir,' Winston said (very bravely, I thought). 'We didn't do it.'

'Fair or not,' said Mr Spratt, 'somebody must know who did do it. It's up to you to come and tell me.' And with that, he swept out of the room.

We were all stunned. We sat there feeling dead depressed, wondering how he would punish us. Would he stop all football matches for the next year? Would he make us come to school on Saturdays? Would he make us write a million essays?

Our teacher, Mr Grimethorpe, (who suffers from stress) looked very worried.

'Terrible news. Terrible news,' he said, shaking his head.

That's when Tod stood up and said, 'Don't worry, Mr Grimethorpe. We'll soon find out who did it.'

Mr Grimethorpe sighed. 'And how will you do that, Tod?'

'We've got Damian. It won't take him long to track down this criminal.'

The eyes of the whole class were on me.

'That depends,' I said mysteriously. 'I'll have to check out the crime scene, look for clues – that sort of stuff. It could take ages.'

The kids started to ask all kinds of questions – 'Where will you look first?' 'How do you know a clue when you see it?' 'What if the criminal's dangerous?'

They went on and on until Mr Grimethorpe clapped his hands for quiet.

After that, our class spent ages discussing graffiti – which was dead good as it meant we weren't doing any maths. But, just as it was getting interesting, Mr Grimethorpe decided we ought to get on with our work.

I wasn't keen on maths. 'If you like, I'll go and take a look at the crime scene now,' I said.

'Not until you've finished your sums,

Damian.'

'But I need to look for clues as soon as possible.'

Mr Grimethorpe gave me a funny look and his cheeks went pink. 'It can wait, Damian. Get on with your work.'

I didn't think this was a good idea. All this time, the crime scene was going cold?* But I was determined to go and examine the graffiti.

I put my head down on the desk, pretending to write. Two minutes later, I stood up, hopping from one foot to the other and waving my hand in the air until Mr Grimethorpe saw me.

'What is it, Damian?'

'I need to go to the toilet, sir,' I said.

Mr Grimethorpe frowned. 'You're making it up,' he said.

I was shocked. 'Honest. I can't wait. I'm desperate.'

*This is a term detectives use and means that the longer a crime scene is left, the more likely that clues will disappear 'cos people trample all over them. That's why detectives have to move fast.

He didn't look pleased. 'Oh very well. But don't be long.'

'I won't,' I said, heading for the door. Before I opened it, I turned.

'Can Winston come with me? I... I'm not feeling very well.'

'Certainly not,' said Mr Grimethorpe. 'He's got work to do.'

'What about Harry?'

'Harry has got work to do, too!'

'Tod?'

'NO! NO! NO!' he shouted, slamming his hand on the desk. 'Go now, Damian, and be back in five minutes or you're in trouble.'

Five minutes! That was not much time for one person to check out the graffiti and look for clues. I raced down the corridor and hoped that the crime scene had not been disturbed.

Chapter 2

At dinner time my gang of trainee detectives, Harry, Tod and Winston, were waiting for me.

'What was it like, Damian?'

'Terrible,' I said. 'You've never seen anything like it.'

'Tell us.'

'Well, they wrote GET LOST SPRAT.'

'No!'

'And they spelled "Spratt" with one "T" instead of two and they did their "S"s the wrong way round.'

'Even Lavender can do "S"s,' said Tod, 'and she's only six.'

I had found other clues, too. I pulled a piece of toilet paper out of my pocket, opened it up and showed them some red flakes.

'What's that?' Winston asked.

'Paint,' I said. 'I scraped it off the graffiti. Detectives often do that kind of stuff. It's called forensics.'

'How's that supposed to help?' Winston asked.

'It's obvious. I can tell what kind of paint the criminal used.'

'So?'

'So I'll go and match it up at the paint shop.'

I pulled another piece of paper out of my pocket. This one contained a scraping of green paint.

'See. He used two colours. Now I'm going to go and buy two cans of spray paint, exactly the same.'

'Why?'

'I have a plan.'

I explained it as carefully as I could.

'I will take the paint to the boys' toilets and leave them on the floor.'

They were all standing with their mouths wide open. I could tell that they didn't understand how I was going to solve the crime. But then they weren't fully trained yet.

'You see,' I said, 'when the criminal goes into the loo, he'll spot the cans and think he'd left them there when he did the graffiti. So he'll pick them up and run for it.'

'But how will we know?'

'We will keep watch in the toilets. There are four of us. We'll take it in turns to go. We don't want Mr Grimethorpe getting suspicious.'

Harry was gawping at me. 'You've got to be joking, Damian,' he said.

'That's the stupidest idea I've ever heard. It'll never work.'

'Yeah,' said Winston. 'Anybody could walk in and pick up the cans. It doesn't make them a criminal.'

After that, there was a sort of rebellion. I tried to explain but it was no use. They wouldn't go along with my plan. So I came up with another one. This one was even more brilliant.

'We'll hold a competition,' I said. 'All the kids will have to write something and we'll look out for the one who does "S"s round the wrong way and who can't spell "Spratt". Find the writer and you'll find the kid responsible for the graffiti.'

I had to persuade them that this was our only chance of solving the crime quickly as dinner time ended in twenty minutes.

FANTASTIC COMPETISHUN

ANSWER 2 SIMPLE QUESTUNS
AND WIN A BRILLIANT
★ PRIZE. ★

We carried a table from the art room round the back of the bike shed. I wrote a poster and stuck it on the wall.

'I still don't see how this will work,' said Harry. 'We haven't even got a prize.'

Write the senteses
with the missing wurds

YOU CUD GET _____
IF YOU DON'T HAVE
A MAP
YOUR HEAD TEECHER

'We'll think of that later,' I said. I was busy writing the questions on a large piece of paper.

Notice how I had cunningly tricked them into writing the words that were written on the toilet walls? That was a stroke of genius.

The news about the competition went round the playground like wild fire. Soon we were surrounded by kids dying to enter. We tore pages from our notebooks and gave them a piece. When we ran out of paper, I used my homework exercise book. I could always tell Mr Grimethorpe that I'd lost it.

When they had finished writing, we collected up the papers and then some kid asked, 'What's the prize, Damian?'

I winked. 'You'll just have to wait and see.'

A few of them got a bit difficult. They tried to force me to tell them what it was. But I refused to say.

'You're a cheat,' somebody shouted. 'I bet there isn't a prize.'

After that, it got a bit out of hand.

Some of the lads started a fight and some of the girls joined in. But luckily, the bell went and we had to go inside.

All that mattered was that we had the pieces of paper. The evidence was in the writing and – as every detective knows – the evidence is the important thing. After school, we would check the papers and find out who was guilty of spraying graffiti on the lavatory walls.

Chapter 3

We went round to the park after school. Lavender, who is Tod's sister, came along to help. We sat on the roundabout, looking at the competition entries, checking the writing. Before long, Winston jumped up, waving a paper in the air.

'I've got it!' he yelled. 'This one's got "Spratt" spelled with one "T".'

'Who did it?' Tod asked.

'George Johnson!'

'Cor!' said Harry. 'I always thought he was dead shy.'

'Just a good cover-up,' I explained. 'Criminals are like that.'

Winston passed the paper over and I examined it. But I could tell straight away that George Johnson was not guilty.

'It's not him,' I said.

'Why?'

'Because the "S" is the right way round. The graffiti writer had written his "S"s the wrong way, remember.'

Winston looked disappointed.

'Good try, Winston. But we have to keep looking.'

We carried on. Tod found another

one with the wrong spelling of Spratt. Then Harry. Then Lavender (twice).

I was disgusted. 'Doesn't anybody know how to spell it?' I asked.

In the end, we made a pile of all those who couldn't spell the head teacher's name but who knew how to write an 'S'.

That left fifteen papers to examine. We were exhausted. Luckily, Tod had some crisps in his pocket and we took a break.

When we were ready to begin again, I reminded them of the clues they were looking for. It's just as well to make it clear when you're dealing with trainee detectives.

We had been searching for only a few minutes, when Lavender said, 'I got it, Damian. I got the cwiminal.' She went crazy. She was leaping up and down as if she was on a trampoline.

I went to look at the paper she was waving. She was right. Spratt had one 'T' missing and the 'S' the wrong way round.

'Brilliant!' I said and I looked at the name on the paper. 'Maisy Parker. She's in your class, isn't she, Lavender?'

'Yeth, she ith.'

'I bet you are surprised she's a criminal. I'm surprised she went into the boys' toilets. I'm surprised she could spray those great big letters across the wall. She's only six.'

'Yeth,' said Lavender. 'And she'th my best fwend.'

Then she stuck out her bottom lip and burst into tears.

Apart from Lavender's crying, my brilliant plan had worked just as I expected. I had tracked down the girl who had ruined the newly painted walls.

'I'll have to report her to the head,' I said. 'I expect he'll call the police.'

Lavender wails grew louder and louder. Best friend or not, I would have to tell the head what I had found.

'No, you won't,' said Harry.

I was shocked when he said that. 'What do you mean? We've got hard evidence.'

'Maisy Parker isn't the only one who can't spell and can't write her "S"s.' He held a paper in his hand. 'Here's James O'Boyle's. It's just the same.'

This confused matters. Now there were two suspects – and before long, we found another four.

Lavender stopped crying as soon as she realised that Maisy Parker was no longer the prime suspect. This could only be a good thing as her bawling was giving me a right headache.

'So what now?' asked Tod.

'Well,' said Harry, 'we can't prove any of these six did it. It's hopeless. I'm going home.'

So that was it. They all went.

I stayed there trying to think of

another plan. But it was no good.

I was too exhausted to come up with any new ideas. I decided to go with my first one. The gang thought it was a rubbish idea but I didn't. I would go to the DIY supermarket to match up the paint I had scraped from the walls. It was my only hope.

Chapter 4

As soon as I had seen the graffiti that morning, I knew it had not been done with ordinary paint. (I have a trained eye for that kind of thing.) So when I went into the DIY supermarket, there was only one kind that interested me – spray paint. Of course there was every type of paint you can imagine – stacked high – rows and rows of it – but the spray cans were at the bottom of Aisle 3.

Unfortunately, there was a woman in that aisle stacking shelves. She was wearing a bright yellow sweatshirt with DIY printed on the front. She had her eye on me as soon as I got near to the spray paint.

'Can I help you?' she asked while I was studying the colours and matching them up to the flakes of paint

in my paper.

I shook my head. 'No thanks. I can manage.'

She pretended she had finished her work and walked down the aisle to stand next to me.

'And what would you be doing, buying cans of spray paint?'

I looked at her in a superior sort of way but said nothing.

She stood next to me with her hands on her hips. 'You wouldn't be thinking of doing a bit of graffiti, would you?' she said.

Well, I was furious. 'No, I wouldn't,' I said. 'I'm buying some paint for my mum, if you must know. She wants to paint our kitchen cupboards.'

'Red and green? That's a bit bright.'

'It's the latest thing,' I said.

But she didn't believe me.

'You're rather young to be here on your own, aren't you?' she said, narrowing her eyes suspiciously. I had had enough! I was about to grab the paint and make a run for it when Mr Robertson came round the corner, pushing a trolley full of wallpaper and stuff.

'Hello, Damian,' he said. 'What are you doing here?'

The DIY woman started on him then. 'Do you know this boy?' she snapped.

Mr Robertson is a great guy. He just smiled and said, 'Yes, I know Damian. He lives next door to me.'

'Does he indeed?' she said in a very sniffy voice. 'Well, I think he was trying to steal some cans of paint.' She leaned forward in a sneaky kind of way and said, 'I suspect that he's one of those

children who goes around spraying
graffiti on walls.'

You should have seen Mr Robertson's
face. He was really mad.

'Damian? Graffiti? Certainly not! I'm
sure he's got a very good reason for
wanting to buy the paint.' He turned
away from the woman and said, 'Pick
up the cans you need, Damian, and
we'll go to the checkout. We're not

going to stand here to be insulted.'

'Right,' I said as I reached for the paint. 'Mum's at home waiting for this.' It wasn't actually true but the DIY woman didn't know that. She shouldn't have accused me of stealing, that's what I say.

I gave her one of my special innocent smiles and walked away, following Mr Robertson and his trolley.

It wasn't until we were standing in the queue at the checkout that I realised that I hadn't any money. What could I do? I couldn't let my plan fail at this stage.

My brain went into top gear and it didn't take long to come up with a brilliant idea.

'Oh no!' I said quite loudly. Then, 'OH NO!' even louder.

Mr Robertson, who was taking the

wallpaper out of his trolley, turned round to see what was the matter. 'Is something wrong, Damian?'

I stood there feeling around in my pockets. 'I've got a hole and my money's fallen out.' I shook my head and frowned. 'It's my fault. I should have noticed. Now I can't pay for the paint.'

Mr Robertson smiled. 'No problem, son. I'll pay. You can give it me back when you get home.'

My cunning plan had worked. 'That's great! Thanks, Mr Robertson.' Then I said, 'But you won't mention it to Mum, will you? She'll get upset if she knows I've lost the money she gave me.'

'Trust me,' said Mr Robertson and he winked. 'I promise I won't say a word.'

When I got home, Mum was in one

of her bad moods – just because I was a few minutes later than usual.

'Where have you been, Damian?' she kept saying. 'Why are you so late? What have you been up to?'

But I had to keep my mouth zipped. Any information leak could ruin the whole operation.

Apart from the Mum problem, I was chuffed that things were going well. Now I had the paint, everything was on course to solve the graffiti crime. I only had to wait until tomorrow morning to put the plan into action.

Chapter 5

Things happened faster than I expected. I got to school early (with the cans of paint in my pockets, of course), only to find that the police were there before me. There was a car in the drive and a policewoman was trying to cordon off the teachers' car park with yellow tape.

I thought I'd better check out what was going on, so I walked in through the main gate.

'I'm Damian Drooth, ace detective,' I said flashing my detective's badge. 'Is this a crime scene?' She hardly looked at the badge.

She wasn't interested. Maybe I

needed to make a new one. The cardboard was beginning to curl at the edges.

'Shouldn't you be in school?' she said.

'I'm very experienced in solving crimes. I might be able to help.'

She raised one eyebrow and smirked. 'I don't think so,' she said. 'Now please go and play your detective games in the playground.'

I get really mad when people treat me like a kid. But she was probably new to the area and didn't know I was a local hero. Inspector Crockitt should inform new officers, if you ask me.

I could see that there was no point in talking to her, so I pretended to walk away – but I cleverly slipped round the back and approached the car park from the other end.

What I saw shocked me rigid!

There was the head's car – silver and shiny and brand new – and SPRAT GO HOME had been sprayed in red paint along the side. This was disgusting! Not only had someone messed up the head's car, they couldn't even spell his name properly. It was probably done by the same boy who had sprayed the lavatory wall.

On the bonnet, it was even worse. There was a terrible drawing of Mr

Spratt's face – cross-eyed with Dracula fangs painted in green. This was serious graffiti. The head must be hopping mad. No wonder he had dialled 999.

Without being seen by the policewoman, I sneaked right up to the car to do some tests. First, I touched the

bonnet and found that the green paint was still wet. Bingo! The criminal couldn't be far away.

Next, I hurried along to look at the red writing. Still wet. Then I stumbled on the most important clue of all. A footprint in red paint. I couldn't believe my luck! But it was crucial that I made a sketch of it.

I had used all the pages in my notebook for the handwriting competition, so I had to think of something else to use. Luckily, my school shirt was white and so I pulled out the front, spread it on the car and did a quick sketch on that.

I had just finished and was putting my pen back in my pocket, when I felt a hand clamp on my shoulder.

'What exactly do you think you are doing?' he said. 'Hoping to do some more graffiti?'

I spun round to see a large policeman

with mean eyes. Another one!

'I'm Damian Drooth, ace detective,' I explained. 'And I'm here to help you solve the graffiti crime.'

He gave a loud, sarcastic laugh as if he didn't believe me. 'You'd better come with me, my lad. We'll see what the head teacher has got to say about you.'

He practically dragged me

into school and down the corridor to Mr Spratt's office. I was furious.

'I think I've got the culprit, sir,' the policeman said as he shoved me through the door.

The head, who was sitting at his desk, looked up. When he saw me, his jaw dropped. I guessed he was shocked to see that the school's most famous pupil had been arrested. I waited for him to shout something like, 'You've made a terrible mistake, constable!' But he didn't.

Instead, he said, 'Damian Drooth! So it was you who sprayed my car!'

I was stunned. How could he think that I – an upholder of the Law – could do such a thing?

'No!' I said. 'I didn't…'

The policeman grabbed hold of my hands and held them out for Mr Spratt to see. 'Just look, sir. There's paint all over him. Isn't that the same as the paint that's been sprayed on your car?'

The head nodded gravely. 'I'm afraid it is,' he said.

It was true that I had a small amount of red and green paint on my fingers – and just a bit down the front of my shirt – but couldn't they understand that I had got it while searching for clues?

I turned round to explain this to the policeman but as I did so, one of the cans of paint fell out of my pocket.

'Aha!' he said. He whipped out some rubber gloves, picked up the can and put it in a plastic bag. 'More evidence.'

Mr Spratt stood up. 'We shall have to send for his mother before you can take him away, constable. We'll find a room where he can wait until she arrives.'

He looked at me, his mouth

drooping at the corners. 'This is a sad, sad day for the school, Damian.'

And that was how I came to be locked away in the medical room wondering how I could escape and find the real culprit.

Chapter 6

The security in our school was less than perfect. It was dead easy to unlock the window and open it. But as it was quite high up, I didn't like the idea of dropping onto the concrete breaking both legs and possibly an arm. No way.

Luckily, while I was hanging out and planning what to do, Harry and Winston came running through the school gates. I cleverly made the sound of an owl to attract their attention. Spies do this when they don't want anybody to notice them. But Harry and Winston weren't listening out for owls so they didn't even look my way.

In the end, I had to yell, 'HARRY! WINSTON! OVER HERE!'

They came running to the window.

'What are you doing, Damian?'

'Trying to escape. I've been locked in the medical room.'

'Why's that?'

'They think I did the graffiti. They'll probably put me in prison.'

'Cor!'

'Give me a hand to get down, will you?'

Harry didn't look pleased. 'We're late for school already and it's assembly this morning.'

'A few more minutes won't hurt,' I said.

I got them to stand under the window with their arms spread against the wall. Then I slithered out and put my feet on their shoulders.

It worked quite well until Winston's knees collapsed and we landed in a heap. But, apart from a tear in my trousers, there was no damage.

'Now you can smuggle me into the hall and I'll announce the name of the real villain to the whole school.'

'Do you know it?'

'No, but I soon will.'

I had been smart enough to borrow a white overall from the medical room by way of a disguise. Once I'd put on my shades and cap, no one would recognise me as I walked between Harry and Winston towards the hall door.

It was bad luck that the policeman arrived with Mum right at that very minute.

'DAMIAN!' Mum screeched. 'WHAT DO YOU THINK YOU'RE DOING?'

'Run for it!' I said.

I raced across the playground and burst into the hall, followed by Harry, Winston, Mum and the policeman.

Mr Spratt was giving one of his boring speeches. I think he should have been a vicar so that he could give sermons any time he felt like it.

Next to him was Inspector Crockitt. I guessed he was here to talk to the kids about the crime of spraying paint.

'Damian Drooth!' shouted Mr Spratt. 'How did you get out? Mr Grimethorpe, take him back to the medical room at once.'

But Inspector Crockitt cut in. 'Let him stay and tell us why he's here, Mr Spratt. In my experience, Damian has a unique approach to crime.'

It was good to hear a senior police officer talking sense. I stepped forward to the front of the hall.

'I know who has been doing all this graffiti,' I announced. 'I have the evidence here.'

I pulled out the front of my shirt so they could see the drawing of the footprint. There were gasps all round the hall. Even Inspector Crockitt looked amazed.

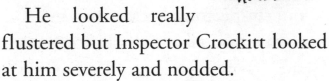

I turned to the head. 'I would like to see the sole of everybody's shoes,' I said.

He looked really flustered but Inspector Crockitt looked at him severely and nodded.

'Oh very well,' said Mr Spratt. 'Children, please stretch your legs out so that we can see the bottom of your shoes.'

It didn't take long. I spotted it straight away. 'Ainsley Scott,' I shouted. 'You are the culprit.'

The soles of his trainers matched my sketch. Not only that, one of them was covered in red paint.

Ainsley knew the game was up and he tried to escape. He leapt up and ran for the door, but Tod, Harry and

Winston were too fast for him. They rugby tackled him and brought him down before anybody else could get near.

The graffiti crime had been solved.

Chapter 7

Back in the head teacher's office, I continued my conversation with Inspector Crockitt. Of course, he would need more proof than some red paint on Ainsley's shoe and a sketch on my shirt.

'I've got something else,' I said.

I pulled the six competition entries out of my pocket.

'What's this, Damian?'

I explained. 'We did a cunning writing test yesterday. Here are the ones that matched the graffiti. This is all the evidence you'll need.'

He was flabbergasted when I handed him the papers. He flicked through them, looking at the names on each one.

'Here's Ainsley Scott's!' he said.

'You're right! He can't spell 'Spratt' and he doesn't know how to write an 'S'. Good work, Damian.'

Sometimes the police need a bit of help in solving crimes. I do my best.

But the police weren't the only ones who were grateful. 'You're a credit to the school,' Mr Spratt said – or something similar.

He gave me a box of Dairy Chox (my favourites) as a 'thank you' and I was looking forward to eating them when I got home. I planned to save the caramels for the others – after all, they did help.

But the kids who had entered the competition were in a bad mood.

'What about the prize?' they bleated. 'You promised there'd be a prize.'

I tried to put them off but it got quite nasty. They were shouting and poking and pestering me so in the end, I said, 'Maisy Parker is the winner and the prize is a box of chocolates.'

That shut them up. Maisy was Lavender's best friend. I had no choice but to hand her the chocolates.

'Oh, thank you, Damian. I've never won a pwize before.'

She was a nice kid. I wondered if she

would like to train with the rest of the gang.

'You can come to the shed, if you like, Maisy,' I said.

'Can I weely, Damian?' she said. 'Can I be a detective like Lavender?'

'We'll see,' I said. 'We're all meeting after school to discuss the graffiti case. Bring your chocolates. New members of the Detective Club always bring something to eat. It's traditional.'

Maisy was pleased to be invited.

Lavender was pleased to have her best friend in the gang.

Harry, Tod and Winston were pleased that the crime was solved.

Only Mum was in a temper.

'How do you do it, Damian?' she moaned. 'Just look at your trousers. They're ripped right down the leg. And your new school shirt is covered in paint. It's ruined! Ruined! Why can't you stay out of trouble?'

I often wonder if Mum will ever recognise her son's true genius.

Maybe one day.

Maybe.